The Return of the Jabberwock

'For the magnificent seven; Jazz, Amber, Noah,
Oakie, Jemima, Isis & Isadora.'
Oakley Graham

TOP THAT

Licensed exclusively to Top That Publishing Ltd
Tide Mill Way, Woodbridge, Suffolk, IP12 1AP, UK
www.topthatpublishing.com
Copyright © 2014 Tide Mill Media
All rights reserved
2 4 6 8 9 7 5 3 1
Printed and bound in China

Illustrated by David Neale
Written by Oakley Graham

ISBN 978-1-78244-222-6

A catalogue record for this book is available from the British Library

Jabberwocky

'Twas brillig, and the slithy toves
Did gyre and gimble in the wabe;
All mimsy were the borogoves,
And the mome raths outgrabe.

'Beware the Jabberwock, my son!
The jaws that bite, the claws that catch!
Beware the Jubjub bird, and shun
The frumious Bandersnatch!'

He took his vorpal sword in hand:
Long time the manxome foe he sought
So rested he by the Tumtum tree,
And stood awhile in thought.

And, as in uffish thought he stood,
The Jabberwock, with eyes of flame,
Came whiffling through the tulgey wood,
And burbled as it came!

One, two! One, two! And through and through
The vorpal blade went snicker-snack!
He left it dead, and with its head
He went galumphing back.

'And has thou slain the Jabberwock?
Come to my arms, my beamish boy!
O frabjous day! Callooh! Callay!'
He chortled in his joy.

'Twas brillig, and the slithy toves
Did gyre and gimble in the wabe;
All mimsy were the borogoves,
And the mome raths outgrabe.

Lewis Carroll, 1872

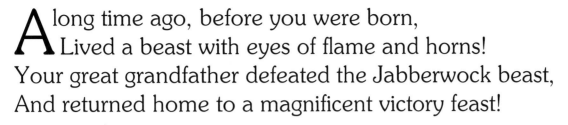

A long time ago, before you were born,
Lived a beast with eyes of flame and horns!
Your great grandfather defeated the Jabberwock beast,
And returned home to a magnificent victory feast!

'I'm going to find my own Jabberwock!' the little boy said,
As he marched past his dad towards the garden shed.
'I'll need a sword and helmet for my big adventure.
Then into Tulgey Wood I'll venture!'

The boy bravely marched through Tulgey Wood,
To find a Jabberwock; oh how he wished he could!
He tried to remember the words his father said,
When he saw something move in the trees ahead …

It had long, spidery legs and horns askew,
Hiding in the shadows, just out of view.
It got closer and closer – it was covered in hair!
What was this strange creature out from its lair?

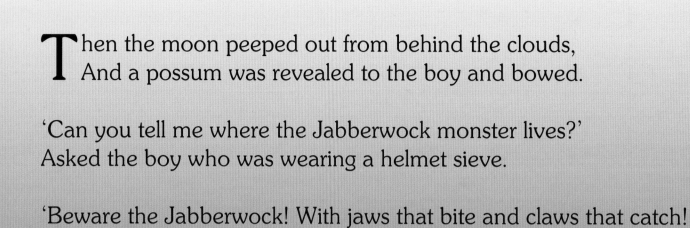

Then the moon peeped out from behind the clouds,
And a possum was revealed to the boy and bowed.

'Can you tell me where the Jabberwock monster lives?'
Asked the boy who was wearing a helmet sieve.

'Beware the Jabberwock! With jaws that bite and claws that catch!
Beware the Jubjub bird and the ferocious Bandersnatch!'

The brave boy continued on his adventure,
And deeper into Tulgey Wood he ventured.
Soon the boy was lost and filled with dread,
When a scary shadow appeared overhead …

It had an ugly beak and a toothless smile,
And it perched in a nest by an old sundial.
The boy started to tremble; the adventure felt real.
Would he end up as the creature's next meal?

The boy reached into his bag and pulled out a torch,
And shone the beam at the shadow, making it … squawk!
A toucan was all that the torch did reveal,
Not a hideous monster eating snippets of veal!

'Why can't I find a Jabberwock to behead?'
Said the boy as he heard a strange noise up ahead.
Then a turtle-like creature appeared in the dark,
It had the ears of a hog and the mouth of a shark!

Just as the boy reached the monstrous creature,
Lightning lit up the sky illuminating its features.
No monster could be seen, just a pig in its place,
Another dead end on the Jabberwock chase!

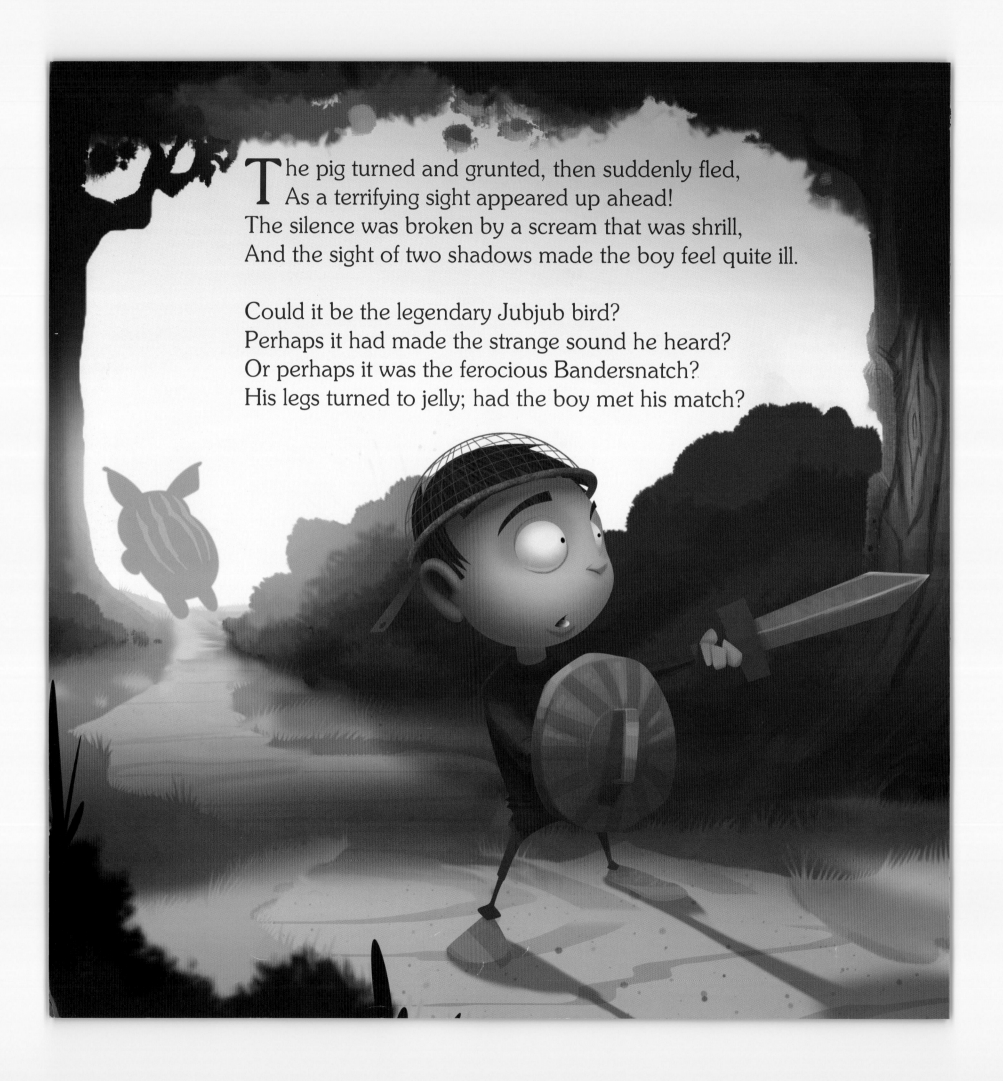

The pig turned and grunted, then suddenly fled,
As a terrifying sight appeared up ahead!
The silence was broken by a scream that was shrill,
And the sight of two shadows made the boy feel quite ill.

Could it be the legendary Jubjub bird?
Perhaps it had made the strange sound he heard?
Or perhaps it was the ferocious Bandersnatch?
His legs turned to jelly; had the boy met his match?

The boy held up his sword; not knowing what to do,
When the lights from a car illuminated the view.
In place of the Jubjub bird and Bandersnatch,
Stood a fox and a heron, stopped dead in their tracks.

The boy was getting tired; he was ready for bed,
And was starting to doubt what his father had said.
He asked the fox and heron, if they happened to know,
Where the Jabberwock lived and which direction to go.

'The Jabberwock lives close by,' the fox said,
As he winked to the heron and pointed his head.
The boy rested for a while by a Tumtum tree,
And recited the poem of the Jabberwocky.

Then out came a creature with eyes of flame,
Whiffling and burbling from the place whence it came!

The boy took one look and as fast as he could …

... ran right back through all of Tulgey Wood!